ELLA
Diaries

TOP SECRET!

Meredith Costain

With thanks to the Gold Street Primary School Reading Club – Miette, Aristea, Esther, Alicia, Kitty, Zac, Robert, Eugenie, Lara, Chloe, Lucy, Annie, Claire, Shey-Lee, Greta and Gen, and also Jacob and Antigone, for their fantabulously fabulous ideas!—M.C.

For our beautiful girls Jade and Zoe—D.M.

Danielle McDonald

Scholastic Australia
345 Pacific Highway Lindfield NSW 2070
An imprint of Scholastic Australia Pty Limited
PO Box 579 Gosford NSW 2250
ABN 11 000 614 577
www.scholastic.com.au

Part of the Scholastic Group
Sydney • Auckland • New York • Toronto • London • Mexico City
• New Delhi • Hong Kong • Buenos Aires • Puerto Rico

Published by Scholastic Australia in 2015.

National Library of Australia Cataloguing-in-Publication entry

Author: Costain, Meredith, 1955- author.
Title: Double dare you / Meredith Costain; Danielle McDonald, illustrator.
ISBN: 978-93-5275-542-4 (paperback)
Target Audience: For primary school age.
Subjects: Diaries--Juvenile fiction.
Schools--Juvenile fiction.
Other Authors/Contributors: McDonald, Danielle, illustrator.
Dewey Number: A823.3

Typeset in Sweetie Pie.
Reprinted by Scholastic India Pvt. Ltd. September 2023
Printed in India at Ram Printograph Delhi

Double Dare You

Monday, after dinner

~~Dear Diary,~~

~~Hello Diary. My name's Ella and~~

~~Once upon a time there was a girl called Ella. She lived~~

How are you supposed to start a diary? I've never had one before. Mum and Dad gave me this one for Christmas because

a) I like writing. I'm always writing stories and they love the poems I make up for their birthdays and other special days.

Inside
of CARD
Dad
To Dad,
You're the best
My favourite relly
Even though
Your socks are smelly!
Happy Father's Day
with love from Ella x x x

b) They think I have a good imagination and they think writing something every day is a good way to 'exercise' it.

c) I'm going into **Grade 5** this year (starting tomorrow!) and Dad says Grade 5 was the **best year of his life**. He thinks I should write down all the things that happen each day so that when I'm an oldie like him I can look back and remember all the amazing and fun things I did over the year.

Well, that's what they think, anyway. My best friend Zoe has a diary, and she says that you can tell it all your secrets and stuff about how you feel, like when something makes you sad or angry.

I'm going to tell you absolutely everything, Dearest Diary. But trust me—I'd never let anyone else get their hands on you . . . EVER.

So, here's my first secret, and only you will know. I'm, um . . . a little bit nervous about going back to school tomorrow. Phew, I said it! We've got a new teacher this year. What if we don't get on? Or she wants us to spend the whole year doing maths problems or boring stuff like the names of rivers and capital cities?

2 x 2 = too boring!

Mr Zugaro, my teacher last year, was amazing. We made up our own plays and acted them out and wrote all kinds of stories.

He even showed us lots of different ways to write poems, which I love! ♥♥♥♥♥♥♥♥

And now I write them all the time. Here, in my room—not just for school. I guess you could call me a **SECRET scribbler.**

Oops! My little sister Olivia just came in but I managed to hide you under my pillow just in time. When it comes to people I don't want reading my diary, Olivia is at the top of my list.

LIST of BANNED people:

1. OLIVIA

2. Mum

3. 

Dad

4. 

⇦ Max

5. ~~Peach~~

TOP SECRET!

KEEP OUT!

Tuesday, straight after school

Hi Diary, (hope you didn't miss me) 

Eek! Today was the worst day of my life. **I am still shaking, see!** It should have been a really good day. Even though it can be scary, there's something really special about the first day of school. I love the smell of new books and pencils and seeing all my friends again and everyone's always happy and smiley after weeks and weeks of summer holidays.

Plus I was really excited because our new teacher, Ms Weiss, has what Nanna Kate calls 'personal style'. Her outfit was TRULY inspired.

Nanna Kate's always telling me I have great 'personal style' as well. I like trying out different combinations of clothes too. Like

(pretty AND practical)

and

(sooo super stylish).

PLUS—and this is the best bit—Ms Weiss is really into creative writing too!!! I can tell we are going to get along just fine.

As soon as the first bell went, all the kids in my new class lined up outside our room. Some of my old **Year 4 FRIENDS** were there, like

And there were some new kids from the other classes as well. When Mr Zugaro told us they were going to mix everyone up, I was really worried that they might split up Zoe and me. Zoe's been my **Best Friend since For Ever.**

THINGS ZOE AND I LIKE DOING TOGETHER

* Swapping secrets
* Sleepovers (no brothers—big OR little—allowed!)

* Music and dancing (especially when we invent our own moves)
* Decorating cupcakes

* Designing stylish outfit combos

But it was OK. We were safe. Mr Zugaro showed us the list with our names on it. Zoe and I were definitely in the same class.

So far, everything was perfect.

So I wasn't expecting everything to go so **horribly wrong**.

Zoe didn't turn up. Not even when Ms Weiss unlocked the door and we all started finding tables to sit at. This is really important because everyone knows that the table you choose on the first day will become your table for the **WHOLE YEAR**.

Unless there are what my Nanna Kate calls

UNFORESEEN CIRCUMSTANCES.

1. Like a fridge falling out of an aeroplane, then dropping down through the roof into your classroom and smashing your table into smithereens.

2. Or a herd of angry elephants picking up your table with their trunks and hurling it out the window as they rampage past.

I'm pretty sure either of these things happening would mean you could move to a different table. But just in case they didn't I figured it would be wise to choose carefully the ~~minute~~ nano-second we entered the classroom.

So I grabbed a table near the window (my favourite place to sit)

THINGS I LIKE TO LOOK AT OUT THE WINDOW

1. trees

2. birds

3. trees with birds in them

4. praying mantises

and waited for Zoe to arrive.

And waited.

And waited.

And waited.

No Zoe.

By now everyone else in the room had paired up. Maryam was sitting next to Sofie. Peter was sitting next to Raf. Even Cordelia, who usually prefers her own space, was sitting next to someone!

Everyone had a friend to sit next to, except me.

Some of the kids who'd come from the other classes were staring and whispering about me, sitting all alone at my table. I knew just what they were thinking. That girl doesn't have any friends. That girl is a **BIG LOSER**.

Still no Zoe.

Ms Weiss asked us all to 'settle down please' then started calling out the names on the roll. She was just up to Sofie's name when I saw the handle turning on the classroom door.

Zoe! I thought.

At last!

The door opened and a girl strolled into the room. Only it wasn't Zoe.

It was Peach.

Peach Parker. What was she doing in here? Remember that list I told you about? The one with Zoe's and my name on it? Well, Peach's name *wasn't* on it. I remember doing a happy dance in my head when I realised I wouldn't have to share a classroom with her any more. Which means she wouldn't be able to [redacted] ever again.

Ms Weiss welcomed her. She didn't ask her why she'd suddenly turned up late to a class she wasn't even supposed to be in. She just asked Peach to find a seat quickly so we could get started.

Peach looked over to where Prinny and Jade, her two best friends, sat waving like maniacs at her. But there was no room at their table of course. There was only one spare seat in the whole room, and we already know where that was, don't we?

Next to me.

I frantically piled all my books and pencil cases and project folders on the table in front of the empty chair so there was no room left for anyone else. Not even a very small dog that might have accidentally wandered into the room which would be excellent because apart from praying mantises, dogs are my favourite animal.

If Zoe wasn't ever coming back, I would be very happy to share my table with a dog. Even Bob, our golden retriever, who is VERY large. And very licky.

But it was no use. Ms Weiss told Peach to sit at my table anyway.

The next bit is too painful and horrible and icky for me to write about right now. It's going to have to wait until tomorrow. Or maybe next year. Or maybe even next century.

Wednesday morning, before school

~~Good~~ Bad morning, Diary,

I woke up really early and now I can't get back to sleep. I don't really want to go back to sleep anyway in case I have another bad dream.

In my dream I was being chased by a

GIANT piece OF FRUIT.

It had long blonde hair and big blue eyes and it chased me right up to the edge of a cliff. If I go back to sleep, it might chase me over the top until I

f
a
l
l

into the swamp at the bottom of the cliff and get all mashed up and eaten by swamp monsters.

So I'm going to write about what happened yesterday instead.

WARNING: If you don't like horror stories, **STOP READING NOW.**

So Peach and I were both sitting at the table, as far away from each other as we could get. Peach kept turning around to make faces at her friends whenever Ms Weiss was writing something on the board, and I kept looking out the window, in the hope that one of

the planes flying overhead might drop a fridge on our table. Then Ms Weiss would have to shift us after all.

Only none of that happened. The planes kept flying right on by, no fridges fell out, and our table stayed exactly where it was.

Peach didn't say **ONE WORD** to me for the entire morning. Not even when Ms Weiss gave us a project to do in pairs. I can't believe it. Ms Weiss is expecting me to do a project about Adventures in Ancient Lands with **Peach!!!!** She obviously doesn't know anything about **WHAT HAPPENED LAST YEAR**.

Instead, Peach took out her perfect pencil case* and Deluxe Set of gel and glitter pens** and started writing down her ideas in her ultra-neat handwriting. All hunched over with her arm hooked around her folder of course, so I couldn't see what she was writing. AS IF I CARE!

* which is EXACTLY like the one I wanted Mum to get me for Christmas, except she didn't, even though I dropped some VERY big hints and left the STATIONERY'R'US catalogue lying around in very conspicuous

places. Like inside her cereal bowl.

** another very important item on my gift wish list.

When the bell went for recess, Peach, Prinny and Jade went out to the playground, arm in arm. They kept looking over at me while I was playing downball with Maryam and Sofie and whispering and giggling, like they knew something I didn't know. But I just ignored them, and went right on playing

DOWNBALL

I played downball at lunchtime too, along with most of the other kids in our class. I kept hoping Zoe would turn up but she didn't. She still wasn't there when we went back in after lunch either.

But Peach was.

And she did her best to get me into trouble with Ms Weiss every chance she could.

She waited till Ms Weiss was writing on the board again, then did a really big, loud stinky burp.

Ms Weiss turned around with a shocked look on her face and said, 'Oooo, manners!' Peach looked straight at me and said, 'Ewww. What did you do *that* for?' as though I was the one who'd burped! Then she put her hand up and said, 'Excuse me, Ms Weiss, would you like me to go to the office and get the air freshener?'

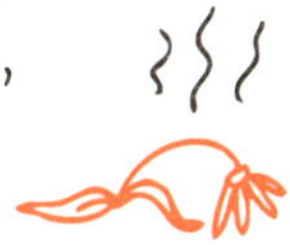

Ms Weiss said, 'That's really thoughtful of you, Peach, but I think we'll be fine for now.' And then she added Peach's name to the STUDENT STARS section of the board, for being so helpful. She didn't say anything to me but I could tell by the look on her face that she definitely thought I'd done the burp.

Then later on Peach passed a note to Prinny and Ms Weiss caught Prinny and Jade giggling over it. She asked them to read out what the note said. They made a big fuss at first about doing that, and then they read it aloud in **REALLY ANNOYING** voices.

> Ms Weiss is weird. She looks like a birthday cake.
>
> Signed: Ella
>
> PS Pass it on

Everyone turned around and stared at me. Peach was staring the hardest, like she was shocked that she was sitting next to someone who could write something like that.

Ms Weiss looked straight at me and said (in a really quiet, sad, desolate* voice): 'Did you write this, Ella?'

* The type of voice princesses use when their knights in shining armour have deserted them in high towers with no steps.

I went as red as Ms Weiss's dress. Then I looked down at the table and shook my head. 'No, Ms Weiss,' I whispered.

But I don't think she believed me. Not after the burp.

Ms Weiss asked Prinny for the note. She crumpled it up and threw it **INto the Bin.** She made a speech, to the whole class, in a very serious voice about how it was wrong to say mean things about other people. Then she told us all to work without speaking to anyone for the next ten minutes. Ha! Like I'd want to speak to Peach EVER AGAIN.

Why did Zoe have to be away today? If she'd been at school none of these horrible, ugly, detestable things would have happened.

Where is Zoe, anyway? I called her house yesterday afternoon but there was no answer. There still wasn't any answer when I tried again before bedtime. I hope her family hasn't been sucked up into a vortex or something. If they have I'll be stuck with Peach at my table for ever.

My life is ruined. I've lost my best friend. And now lovely, stylish Ms Weiss (who I was sure was going to be my favourite teacher) HATES me!

Reasons Ms Weiss HATES ME

1. She thinks I'm a ~~trub~~ troublemaker.
2. She thinks I don't have any manners.
3. She thinks I'm a (smelly) burper.
4. She thinks I'm making fun of her style (which is so not fair, because I think she is the MOST stylish teacher I have ever had!)

Wednesday, after dinner

Dear amazing, wonderful, fabulous Diary,

Zoe is back!

I am sooo relieved. (Can you tell?) Zoe's family wasn't sucked up into a vortex after all! She was waiting in our special place in the playground when I arrived at school. Her nonna broke her hip early yesterday morning and Zoe's mum had to rush off to the country to look

after her. She took Zoe and her older brother, Will, with her. She said by the time they got home it was too late to call me.

Maybe if she had called I wouldn't have had so many bad dreams about fruit. ☹

I told Zoe all about how Ms Weiss had made Peach sit next to me and how Peach had tricked Ms Weiss into thinking I was a mean note-writing burper. Zoe said sorry about six times and I could tell she really meant it.

That's why she's my best friend. Then she said to fix things we needed to write a petition to Ms Weiss with two aims:

Aim 1. Change Ms Weiss's opinion of me from a negative one to a positive one.

Aim 2. Convince Ms Weiss to let us sit together.

Just as she was telling me the second aim, Ms Weiss walked past us on her way to the staffroom. She was talking to Mr Zugaro so I'm pretty sure she didn't see us. Her outfit today was even more stylish than the one she was wearing yesterday. I was dying to tell her how wonderful she looked, but I didn't in case she thought I was trying to make fun of her again.

AS IF I WOULD!!

Anyway, her tantalising trend-setting outfit gave me an idea for the petition.

Here's what we wrote:

Dear Ms Weiss

You are looking very lovely today. (In fact nothing at all like a birthday cake. I can't believe someone wrote that. Unless it was a really nice one, which ~~ackshertly~~ actually when you think about it, most birthday cakes usually are.) We especially like the way you have teamed a bright red bolero top with a green dress with purple swirls on it and a matching purple flower in your hair.

We also like your earrings.

~~Did they cost a lot of money?~~*

It is very important that my best friend Zoe (who was away yesterday) and I sit together in class this year.

Here are the Reasons WHY

1. Zoe and I have been best friends since forever.
2. It isn't Zoe's fault that she missed out on the first day of school when important decisions like table-choosing are made. She was having a family ~~emurjency~~ emergency.
3. Zoe has a medical ~~condishun~~ condition which means that if she doesn't sit next to a very close friend she will break out into an itchy rash. Which might be catching.
4. I have the same ~~condish~~ condition.
5. ~~If I have to sit next to Peach for even one more minute I will die.~~**

Thank you for considering our request.

Yours truly,

Ella and Zoe

* Zoe made me take this bit out because she said her mum told her it is rude to ask people how much their things cost.

** Zoe made me take this bit out as well. She said we should only write things that are true. But this IS true!

I nearly did chicken out, but Zoe put her arm around me, and smiled at me in a very kind and **SOLID** way, and together we knocked

on the staffroom door and asked for Ms Weiss. We gave her the petition and she read it right there in the doorway in front of us, while all the other teachers nearly knocked her over as they rushed off to their classrooms. I was worried she might be cross (especially because there were so many spelling mistakes, and because of all the bruises she must be getting from all those rushing teachers) but when she finally stopped reading and looked up at us she didn't look cross.

She looked happy. I could tell she was happy because she was laughing. People only laugh when they're happy, right?

Then she told me I was a 'sweetheart' (Me!!!) and she didn't believe I was capable of doing smelly burps when her back was turned, even if other people tried to say I did. (Which means maybe she doesn't hate me after all. Pheww....)

And then she said of course Zoe and I could sit together and she would find somewhere else for Peach to sit. She said there'd been last minute changes to class numbers so there hadn't been enough chairs and tables in the room, but it had all been fixed up now, and to hurry along to our classroom because the bell was about to ring.

And here's the best bit. When we went into our classroom, there was a new table at the front of the room, right in front of Ms Weiss's desk.

And guess who Ms Weiss told to sit at that table?

HINT: Their name rhymes with

Thursday, after school

Hey there, Diary,

Peach hasn't spoken to me since Ms Weiss asked her to sit at the new table. You would think this would be a good thing and mostly it is, but it also makes me a bit nervous and twitchy, in case she is planning something to get me back.

So I wrote this haiku about her.

The volcano sits
Its sides shaking and heaving
Waiting to erupt

Mr Zugaro taught us how to write **haiku** last year. Haiku are Japanese poems about nature. They have three lines and each line has to have five or seven sillybubbles* in it.

* I think that's what they're called.

Friday, before lights out

Hey, Diary-doo,

Nanna Kate is here looking after Olivia and Max and me because Mum and Dad have gone to the movies. They are probably going to sit really close to each other in the back row and hold hands. They might even KISS each other. Ewwwwww. But I am HAPPY, HAPPY, HAPPY because Nanna Kate and I spent TWO WHOLE HOURS going through my wardrobe trying out different outfit combinations. She even let me stay up a whole hour later than I normally do.

Nanna Kate is the BEST Nanna in the WHOLE WILD WORLD.

Good night
Sleep tight
Don't let
Your mean friends bite.

Saturday night, just before dinner

Hello again, Diary,

Mum took me to Parkfields Shoppingtown today to buy me some new trainers for the cross-country event that's coming up soon. I found some purple ones with **pink sparkles** across the toes. They were so **AMAZINGLY ATTRACTIVE** I had to wear them out of the shop.

Cordelia was in the shoe shop buying trainers too. Hers were OK, but not as spectacularly, splendiferously sensational as mine.*

The only bad thing about the day was that Olivia and Max came too, and they spent all their time whingeing and bugging Mum to buy them ice-creams when I'd rather have been looking at FASHION. And guess where Max's ice-cream ended up?

Yep. You got it.

ALL OVER my beautiful new shoes. Little brothers and sisters are SOOO embarrassing!

* As you have probably noticed by now, I like using words that start with the same sound.

Sunday morning, just before lunch

Bob dug his way out under the front fence again and bounced up at Mr Supramaniam when he went past in his motorised wheelchair. Mr Supramaniam got a fright and crashed his wheelchair into our next-door neighbour's fence. And now he is in BIG TROUBLE. (Bob, not Mr Supramaniam. Although I don't think our next-door neighbour is very happy about what Mr Supramaniam did to his fence.)

Have to go now, Mum wants me to set the table for lunch!

Monday, straight after school

Dear Diary,

Roses are red
Praying mantises are green
Precious Peach Parker
Makes me want to SCREAM!

That is all.

Tuesday, after school

G'day, G'Diary,

It's official. There's a new craze at school. Last year it was making loom bands. Everyone (well, except for Cordelia, who's not really into that kind of stuff) sat around in the playground with plastic looms and a rainbow of rubber bands and made friendship bracelets for each other. Peach and Prinny and Jade had so many bracelets it gives me a headache just thinking about how big a number that must be.

The year before that it was elastics, or French skipping—which is what my Nanna Kate used to call it when she was at school about nine hundred years ago. Zoe and Peach* and I used to play it every lunchtime. We chanted rhymes while we were skipping. This one was my favourite:

Henry, Henry (or whoever you
thought was annoying)
Sitting on a pin
How many inches did the pin go in?
One, two, three, four.

Of course you know whose name I would put in the first line now, don't you? ☺

* This was when Peach and I were still best friends, before the mean, terrible, nasty, awful, horrible, dreadful, shocking thing she did to me at the start of last year, which I will never ever EVER forgive her for. Ever.

Anyway, the new craze this year is downball. As soon as the bell goes for recess or lunch there's a big stampede to bags one of the downball courts. There are only six courts so there are always queues of kids waiting for the first four players to go out so they can get into a game.

Today Zoe and I played Peter and Raf.

Zoe was playing like a star, serving up some really hot balls and smashing them around the court. She even threw in a few footsies. Then Peter did a low return that skimmed across the ground. Zoe raced for it but she was too late. The ball double-bounced in her square and she was out. I moved up to King and Sofie went to Dunce.

We stayed in for ages. I could see the kids waiting in the reserves line getting more and more fidgety, waiting for their chance to play. Finally Peter hit a full into Raf's square and went out, which meant he had to go right to the end of the line.

I stayed in though, for the whole of recess. I even did a header!

Downball is the best. You don't have to sit around in little groups all the time, worrying about what people might be saying or thinking about you in other little groups. You get to move around really fast all over the court. I love it.

In fact, I **love** it so much I made up this poem about it.

Playing downball is good fun
Always keeps you on the run
Makes you want to sing and shout
Just make sure you don't go out!

Wednesday, before bedtime

Hey there, Diary,

I **CANNOT** believe what happened at school today.

We were all working on our Adventures in Ancient Lands projects. Zoe and I are doing Ancient Egypt. We've invented a character called Professor Violet Higginbottom, who discovers a secret chamber in a pyramid that has been buried for centuries under the sands of the Egyptian desert. Inside the chamber is the mummified body of an Egyptian pharaoh. And lots of treasure, and those little stone jars they keep all the guts in. And slaves to look after them in the next life, and mummified cats. We're even drawing a map showing the secret passageways inside the pyramid.

Ms Weiss said three people from the class could give a report on how their projects were going. Ms Weiss chose Peter first. He and Raf are writing an adventure starring some of the Greek gods. Then she chose Daisy, who's writing about Ancient China with Grace.

She looked over at our table and I was sure she was going to choose me. Only Peach's hand shot up really high and she said (in that whiny voice she uses when she wants to suck up to teachers): 'Please, Ms Weiss, can Prinny, Jade and I go next? We're just sooo excited about our project.'

Bleuchhh. I was SURE Ms Weiss would roll her eyes around in her head like I was doing. But instead she said, 'Yes, of course, Peach. We'd love to hear all about it, wouldn't we, class?' And then before everyone could call out 'Noooooooooooooo!' she awarded Peach another Student Star for being so refreshingly 'Super Enthusiastic'.

Bleuchhh to the power of ten trillion!!! So Peach stood up and said her group's project was about Ancient Egypt.

Uh-oh, I thought. Surely she's not going to do it again . . .

And then she said they're writing about an explorer who finds a pyramid no-one has ever seen before and inside the pyramid is . . .

You know what's coming next, don't you?

Inside the pyramid is a secret chamber with the mummy of a 'lost' pharaoh in it. Plus all the other things like the treasure and the jars for guts and the slaves and even the mummified cat we're putting inside our secret chamber.

Zoe and I looked at each other with our mouths hanging wide open while Ms Weiss congratulated Peach's team for coming up with such an 'original idea' and awarded them all a Student Star.

Peach looked over at our table and gave us both this really **Fake Smile.** Then she sat down again and started colouring something in with a yellow texta. Probably a map of the secret passageways leading to the secret chambers inside the secret pyramid she copied off us.

Now what are we supposed to do? If we keep going with our project Ms Weiss will think we copied Peach's idea. But if I tell Ms Weiss that Peach copied our idea (I don't know exactly how she did it yet, but she definitely did) then Peach will just deny it and everything will end up in a big mess, **JUST LIKE IT DID LAST TIME***. Zoe and I are going to have to come up with a whole new idea for our project. Why couldn't Peach just stay in the class she was supposed to be in this year?

* I wonder if Peach realises she doesn't need to copy things I write because she's actually a good writer herself. Oops! I just gave away part of the terrible, horrible, bad thing she did. So I might as well tell you what happened.

Last year we both decided to enter a writing competition. I had this brilliant idea for a mystery story with a really cool ending.

I told Peach all about it at recess one day. But when the results of the competition came out, Peach's story won first prize—and it was almost exactly the same as mine! I tried to tell people that Peach had copied my ideas, but she just said I'd copied hers, and I was trying to spread fibs about her. Total betrayal! And that's why we're not best friends any more.

Thursday morning, before school

I had really bad dreams again last night. This time, a volcano was erupting. And big pieces of fruit were shooting out of the top and running down the sides. I tried to run away but it was like my legs were moving through a mass of marshmallow, and I got drenched in icky, sticky sliced fruit.

Thursday, after school

Dearest Diary,

The good news

We played downball again today. As soon as the bell went, Zoe and I ran for the courts to make sure we got a game. And we did. (Sadly, it all goes

downhill

from here.)

The bad news

Peach and her friends were in the reserves queue. They kept calling out stupid things like 'El-la's a Smel-la' and 'Don't be so toe-y, Zoe-y' so we'd mis-hit the ball and go out. My face went a bit red when Peach called me 'a smel-la', but I just ignored her and kept playing.

The badder news

Then Sofie did a really sneaky shot and I hit it out of the court on the full. I was out, so off I went to the back of the queue, just behind Daisy.

The ~~worser~~ ~~worserer~~ even badder news

The line of bored people standing around waiting to play seemed much shorter than when we first started playing. Why? I hear you asking. I did too:

Me: What happened to the kids waiting to play? Half of them are missing.
Daisy (laughing nervously): They . . . er . . . went with Peach.

Me (suspiciously): Went with Peach where?

Daisy (pointing to the big peppercorn tree near the fence): Over there.

Me: And this was because . . .?

Daisy (more nervous laughter): Um . . . it was right after she said, 'Come on, this is a BABIES' GAME for LOSERS. We're out of here.'

Me (looking over at people **I THOUGHT WERE MY FRIENDS** laughing and joking with Peach): Oh.

But secretly I was thinking, Good. I hope they go there next lunchtime too. I don't want to play downball with Precious

Princess Peach Parker AND ANYONE ELSE WHO WANTS TO HANG OUT WITH HER anyway.

Friday, just before dinner

Dear Diary,

Today at school Ms Weic

Sorry about that. Olivia just came into my room and interrupted me, so I had to hide you under my pillow. I don't think she saw you though . . .

Olivia always wants to borrow my stuff. I tell her to get her own stuff and she goes whining off to Mum about it, saying how mean I am. And then Mum says (in that really serious 'Mum' voice she puts on sometimes): 'Now, Ella, you know how important it is to share your things with other people. Especially someone as sweet and kind as your darling little sister.'

Bleuchhh.

How come Olivia never has to share her stuff with me? Then again, who would want to borrow her stuff anyway? All her things are plain, plain, plain.

She would never think of this masterpiece:

She has absolutely NO sense of personal style at all.

Mum's calling me to come and set the table so I have to stop now. We're having spag bol— MY FAVOURITE. Yum!

I'll write more after dinner.

Friday, just after dinner

Sorry, dearest Diary, I'm back.

Something really weird happened at school today. Ms Weiss was in the middle of telling us about how solids, liquids and gases behave when Georgia suddenly stood up and started doing the CHICKEN DANCE. Right in the middle of the classroom! She was flapping her arms and making little beak shapes with her hands and wiggling up and down. She even did a few chicken noises. And then she sat down again, looking straight ahead as though nothing had happened.

Of course everyone started laughing and talking about what we'd just seen, and Ollie and Zac started making B-Burrrkkk! chicken noises of their own. But then Ms Weiss called for quiet and everyone settled down again.

Ms Weiss just smiled at Georgia, and said she hoped she was feeling better soon, and that whatever it was she had wasn't catching. Then she went back to telling us what happens to liquids and gases when you heat them. Everyone kept waiting for Georgia to do the CHICKEN DANCE again, but she didn't. She didn't even make any chicken noises.

Like I said. Weird.

Monday, after school

Greetings, O most excellent Diary of mine.

Guess what happened today. Poppy went up to Jacob Curry (this really popular guy in Grade 6 who's captain of all the sports teams) and **TALKED TO HIM**. Poppy! She's the quietest, shyest girl in our grade. And then at lunchtime, her best friend Chloe started up a conga line of dancers (including Mr Bing and Ms Sneddon, who were both on yard duty at the time) that snaked all around the playground.

Tuesday, after dinner

Hey, Diary,

I'm supposed to be doing my homework but there is so much more important stuff to write about! Today Mr Martini, the principal, found a plastic fake vomit on the windscreen of his car. Peter said he saw him picking it up with a tissue (in case it was real) and throwing it into the bushes.

I'm glad it was fake vomit and not a real one. Even thinking about real vomit makes me feel sick, ever since I stepped in a pool of dog vomit after Bob accidentally got locked in the pantry and chowed his way through six packets of Hot'n'Spicy dry noodles and three packets of instant cupcake mix (with strawberry icing).

Then later, during maths, this happened:

Alysha (squirming around in her chair): Excuse me, Ms Weiss.

Ms Weiss: Yes, Alysha.

Alysha: I'm **BUSTING**. Can I go to the toilet please?

Ms Weiss (looking concerned): Yes, of course you can.

FIVE MINUTES LATER. . .

Alysha (waving hand in the air): Excuse me, Ms Weiss.

Ms Weiss: Yes, Alysha.

Alysha (innocently): I'm busting AGAIN. Can I go to the toilet please?

Ms Weiss (wrinkling her forehead in that way teachers do when they think someone is trying to pull a swifty, but they're not 100% sure): I don't think so, Alysha. You've just been. Wait till recess, please.

FIVE MINUTES LATER . . .

Alysha (waving hand in the air): Excuse me, Ms Weiss.

Ms Weiss (smiling thinly): Yes, Alysha.

Alysha (even more innocently): I'm **STILL** busting. Can I go to the toilet please?

Ms Weiss: No.

And this kept happening every five minutes until the bell went. Alysha **NEVER** does stuff like that!

OK, will stop now and do my maths homework. ☹ ☹ ☹

No . . . wait! I feel a poem coming!

Maths homework
So boring that I'm snoring
Trying . . . sighing . . . crying
Makes me want to **VOMIT!!!**

Wednesday, just before bedtime

Dearest, darlingest Diary,

I've been waiting all day to tell you this, but now I'm not sure that I can, in case it makes me too sad . . . ☹ Oh well, here goes.

It's about our downball games. The line of reserves waiting to play is getting shorter and shorter each day. Today, when I hit another full and had to go to the back of the queue, there were only three kids in front of me. I heard all this laughing coming from over near the peppercorn tree, and surprise, surprise, Peach was there, with her little friends. But also lots of other kids from our class . . . like Alysha and Lily, and Chloe and Poppy . . . sitting in a big circle. Those girls don't even LIKE Peach.

Then, suddenly, Lily stood up and everyone started clapping and chanting:

'Do it! Do it!'

Lily started walking towards the downball courts. I thought she was going to join the queue but she went right past me to the rubbish bin, which was full to the top with stinky lunch leftovers and banana peels. Then Lily bent over and put her face right up close to the bin.

'Do it! Do it!' chanted the crowd.

Lily gave the bin a big sloppy kiss. The kids under the tree stopped chanting 'Do it!' and started cheering instead.

'Yuck!' squealed Lily. 'That was disgusting.' Then she laughed so much I thought her head was going to fall off.

And then I noticed something else. I was the only one left in the queue. All the others had gone to join Peach.

Thursday, straight after school

I have to write about what happened today before I **BURST!!**

When Zoe and I ran over to the downball courts at lunchtime, we were the only ones there. Everyone else was in a big circle under the peppercorn tree, laughing and joking. Even Peter and Raf!

We played two square for a while but it wasn't any fun without the others. We kept stopping and looking over at their stupid circle, wondering what they were all doing.

Things they MIGHT BE DOING IN THE CIRCLE AND reasons WHY OR WHY NOT

	WHY	WHY NOT
1. Playing Murder in the Dark	It's played in a circle	It wasn't dark
2. Playing Drop the Hanky	It's played in a circle	It's a babies' game
3. Playing Duck Duck Goose	It's played in a circle	It's an even babier game

There was only one way to find out.

We were going to have to join them. So we walked over to the peppercorn tree. I made Zoe walk first in case Peach had booby-trapped the path.

As we got closer to the circle we noticed Peach was actually sitting just outside it, on a kind of throne made out of small logs and cushions. Maybe Peach thinks she really is a princess. She was even wearing a crown. (Though it looked just like the cheap, tinny one Olivia wears when she's playing dress-ups with her friend Matilda.)

Peach started being all fakey nice when she saw us standing on the edge of her circle. She reached over and tapped Poppy lightly on the arm, then asked her to move over so we could join in the fun.

And then I noticed something else sitting right in the middle of the circle.

We squeezed in between Poppy and Chloe. Everyone was staring at the shoe, like it had magical powers or was about to turn into a boy wizard or a fire-breathing dragon.

Then Poppy asked Peach if she could have a turn spinning the shoe. But Peach said only Prinny and Jade—**The Official Keepers of the Shoe**—were allowed to do that. Prinny shuffled across into the centre of the circle and picked up the shoe. She held it a few centimetres above the ground then gave it a fast flick with her fingers so that it spun around a few times. It was pretty boring. No flames shot out of it and no-one got turned into a frog. Or even a praying mantis. Everyone started calling out, 'It's landed on Zoe!'

But then I got it. The toe of the shoe was *pointing* at Zoe. She'd been **CHOSEN** by the shoe and now something was going to happen to her.

Peach leaned back on her throne and smiled like a snake*. Then she said:

The shoe has landed
Fair and square
And now you have to
Do a dare.

* I'm not 100% sure that snakes can actually smile, but if they could, they'd look like Peach on her throne.

Aha! So it's a DARING game. Suddenly it all made sense. I was so proud when Zoe smiled back and said, 'Bring it on.'

Zoe's really brave like that. But she probably hadn't realised when she said it that the dares Peach gives out are mostly very silly or embarrassing for the person doing them.

She might change her mind about being brave if she finds out she has to do the budgie dance** in class or kiss the part of Mr Martini's windscreen that the fake (or—EWWW!—real, we never actually found out) vomit was stuck to.

So anyway, after Zoe said to bring it on, Peach said, 'OK, here's what you have to do . . .'

Sorry, Diary, have to go. Mum's calling me!

** The budgie dance is closely related to the chicken dance, only the steps are based on the movements of budgies rather than chickens. Not many people know the steps to this one because Olivia and I made it up in our lounge room one day before she became so annoying.

Friday, after school

Hey there, Diary-O,

Zoe is still really upset. I raided my emergency piggy bank—the one with the sign on it that says:

I bought as many of her favourite chocolate bars as I could from the milk bar on the corner but she says she's never going back to school because she won't be able to face anyone on the sports committee EVER AGAIN.

Here's what happened.

We always have a special sports assembly on Friday mornings where all the house captains give their sports reports. Zoe is captain of the girls' swimming team for our house and she had her speech all prepared. But Zoe's dare was that she had to take out all the people's names, or the names of events, in her speech and replace them with the words 'Grandma's undies'. So this is what her speech sounded like:

> Good morning, Grandma's undies, my name is Grandma's undies and today I am giving you the report about Grandma's undies.

(Everyone was already laughing by this stage but Zoe kept reading, even though her face was as red as our house banner on the wall behind her.)

Last Wednesday, we held the trials for Grandma's undies in the Grandma's undies Memorial Swimming Pool. Twenty-six students from all year levels competed in the following events—Grandma's undies, Grandma's undies, Grandma's undies, and finally, Grandma's undies—in the hope of gaining a place in the house team. The following students were chosen to represent Lawson House: Grandma's undies, Grandma's undies, Grandma's undies, Grandma's undies—and as emergency this year—Grandma's undies.

By this time all the students in the hall were howling with laughter* and some of the Grade 4 boys had fallen off their chairs and were rolling around on the floor.

Even Mr Martini was making these strangled, snorting noises, like he was trying not to laugh but couldn't hold it in any more.

* Howling with laughter is what my Nanna Kate says is the best way to describe the way people laugh when they're laughing really hard, but it sounds like something a wolf would do and I'm not 100% sure that wolves can actually laugh.

Anyway, after that last bit Zoe had to stop reading her report because she said she was too ~~embariss~~ ~~embarruss~~ embarrassed to keep on going. The only way I could cheer her up was by agreeing to play Spin the Shoe again. If it landed on me, I promised

CROSS MY Heart Hope to DIE

that I would do the dare Peach said I had to and not even **THINK** about backing out of it. Because Zoe thinks that any dare Peach sets for me is going to be a trillion times worse than the Grandma's Undies one.

This could all go REALLY, REALLY badly. But it's what best friends do, isn't it? They agree to do difficult things for their friends even though it might mean maximum embarrassment to the power of ~~ten~~ one thousand for them.

BUT (HORROR of horrors to the power of gatrillion) now I have to wait until Monday to find out what Peach's dare is going to be!!!!!

Saturday, before lunch

I'm starting to get really twitchy about the dare Peach is going to give me.

What if she . . .

Saturday, after lunch

No, she wouldn't do that. Would she???

Saturday, before dinner

Or maybe she's going to make me . . .

Saturday, after dinner

I can't bear the suspense any more. I wish Monday would hurry up and come.

Sunday, first thing

NO I DON'T!!!!!

Sunday, before bed

I'm wondering if I draw spots on my tummy with a red texta I'd be able to convince Mum that I had Occhilupo's disease* which has an itchy red rash that is HIGHLY contagious (that means you can catch it

easily from people who already have it) and therefore I won't be able to go to school tomorrow. But that would mean breaking my promise to Zoe and I don't want to do that.

* This disease doesn't actually exist but it sounds like it might, doesn't it? Mum isn't a nurse or a doctor or anything so how would she know that I just made it up

after seeing the name on the back of one of Dad's old surfing magazines from the year 10,000 BC.

Monday, before bedtime

So at lunchtime today Zoe and I took a couple of deep breaths, linked arms, and went back to the circle of kids under the peppercorn tree. (As you can probably tell by now, I decided **NOT** to pretend I had Occhilupo's disease after all and went to school to face Peach's dare instead.) When we got there

Princess Peach was sitting on her throne again, only this time she was wearing a bigger, tinnier crown

with even more fake jewels on it. YAWN. Doesn't she know ANYTHING about regal style??? Obviously NOT.

Prinny and Jade were still the only ones allowed to spin the shoe. It's so obvious that they're totally rigging where it lands. Surely anyone with even a tiny brain in their head knows that. Peach was still the only one who was allowed to give out the dares.

It was Jade's turn to spin the shoe. And surprise, surprise, guess who it landed on.

HINT: Their name rhymes with 'Umbrella'.

I took a deep breath and looked straight at Peach. And then I asked her what my dare was.

Peach gave me another one of her snake smiles and said, 'You know Cordelia, who is in our class?'

And I said, 'Yes, of course I know Cordelia. Everyone knows Cordelia.'

But the whole time I was saying that I was worrying about what Peach was going to dare me to do. Because Cordelia is this really sweet, lovely girl but she's not like anyone else in my year. Most kids go all weird if their best friend is away for even one day (like I did!) but she's quite happy hanging out by herself. She has this great toy furry animal collection and sometimes she brings some of the animals to school and talks to them like they're her friends.

I looked across the playground to the library steps where Cordelia usually spends recess and lunchtimes. She was sitting there reading a book, with Mr Wombat snuggled up on her lap. Everyone knows Mr Wombat is her favourite furry toy.

And then Peach said, 'I dare you to kidnap Mr Wombat from Cordelia when she's not looking and hide him somewhere she can't find him.'

I quickly looked at Zoe, who was waiting for me to keep my promise to her and accept the dare. And then I looked over at Cordelia again, sitting all alone on the library steps. Mr Wombat was the only true friend she had in the whole world.

Peach could see I was wavering about what to do. 'OK,' she said, her eyes going all snaky again. '**DOUBLE DARE YOU**.' Double dares are really hard to refuse. If you back down from a double dare at our school, it means you're chicken. No-one likes other kids to think they're chicken.

Plus Zoe was counting on me as well. It would be superduper easy for me to get Mr Wombat away from Cordelia without her knowing. I even knew about sixty hiding places that she'd never think of looking for him in. Zoe would be happy again and no one would think I was chicken for backing out of a double dare.

#13 pot plant

But then I thought about how Cordelia was going to feel trying to get to sleep that night without her best friend to talk to. And Zoe already has lots of other friends, even if she didn't want to be mine any more.

#29 behind bush

#3 in a toy truck

#46 on a bookshelf

I stood up and went over to where Peach was sitting on her throne.

'Yeah?' I said, looking down at her. 'Well, I don't care if you triple dare me, I'm not going to do it. Cordelia loves Mr Wombat and I'm not going to take him away from her.'

Then I heard all these clapping sounds. Only this time it wasn't the other kids slow-clapping while they chanted, **'Do it! Do it!'**

This time they were just clapping me for standing up to Peach and her silly dares.

Princess Peach stuck her nose in the air. 'Come on,' she said to Prinny and Jade. 'Let's go. I'm bored of this game now anyway.' And they stomped off.

Everyone in the circle just sat there looking at each other, wondering what to do next.

Then two boys ran past, chasing a basketball that had bounced off the court they were playing on. It gave me a really good idea.

I pointed to the rest of the kids on the basketball court, running up and down and shooting baskets. 'Who wants to play basketball?' I asked.

'Me!' yelled all the kids in the circle. Including Zoe.

So that's what we all did. Who knows? Maybe we'll even start a new craze!

Good night, dear Diary.

PS (one week later)

Oh yeah. Remember those projects we were doing? About Adventures in Ancient Lands? Well, the weirdest thing happened. Cordelia's project partner, Joybelle, ended up getting chickenpox (she had bright red spots all over her face and tummy just like people who have Occhilupo's disease would get if it was actually a real disease and not just one I made up) and so Ms Weiss asked her to work with me and Zoe instead.

And **GUESS WHAT!!**

You never will (and I'm tired and want to go to sleep now) so I'll just tell you.

It turns out Cordelia (who reads A LOT of books) knows all this AMAZING stuff about an ancient tribe of warrior women called the Samartians, who rode around on horseback having adventures and fighting battles. So we changed our project to be about that.

And **GUESS WHAT ELSE!!!**

Ms Weiss said our topic was so interesting and original she gave us special bonus points, and our team project WON!!

Guess who wasn't very happy about that????

HINT: Her name rhymes with leech.

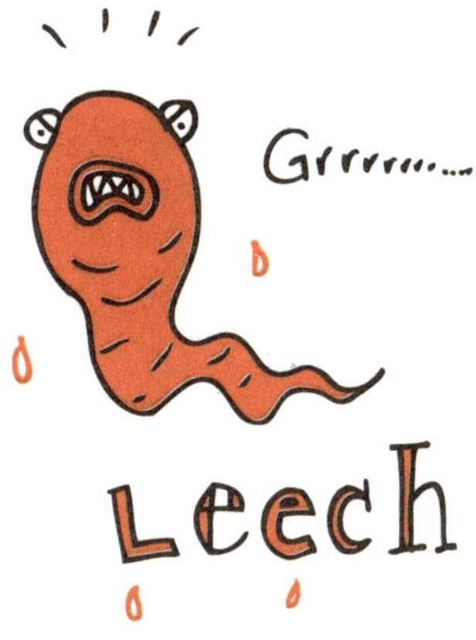

CLASS 5 W

Adventures in Ancient Lands Project

BEST TEAM

ELLA, ZOE and CORDELIA

Ms E. Weiss

MS E. WEISS

PPS (two weeks later)

And remember how I said basketball might become our new craze?

Well, I must have psychic powers or something, because IT DID!!! Only we call it B-Ball.

Zoe and I (and just about everyone else in our class, except for You Know Who x 3) race over to the B-Ball courts as soon as the bell rings. Zoe and Peter are the best goal shooters and Cordelia is the umpire (she learnt the rules from a book in the library). And Mr Wombat is our mascot! He sits on the sidelines and watches every game. Sometimes he even helps out Cordelia with difficult umpiring decisions.

I love B-Ball so much I wrote this song about it.

B-Ball

B-Ball, B-Ball
You're the best
Play it when
You're feeling stressed
Shooting baskets
All day long
Join me in
My B-Ball song!

B-Ball 4 EVER. YEAH!!!!

Make your own diary!

Put a photo of you in the below frame and write your name in the oval!

Top 10 things you LOVE to do:

1. Draw and crayt
2. Make secret clubs
3. Write birthday poems
4. play with my friends
5.
6.
7.
8.
9.
10.

Write your own haiku!

Haiku are Japanese poems about nature. They have three lines and each line has to have five or seven syllables in it.

Draw the funkiest fashion you can imagine!

SNEAK PEEK

Ballet Backflip

Saturday, before dinner

Dear Diary,

You will never ever EVER believe what happened today!

I was at ballet class like I normally am every Saturday morning. My ballet class is held at:

(which is just a fancy way of saying Mrs Fry's ballet school). Except, actually, the school isn't very fancy at all.

The main reason for this is because ballet is held in our local scout hall. Which means when we're not there, the scouts are. Which is a VERY BAD THING.

Reasons why sharing YOUR SPACE with SCOUTS is BAD:

1. Scouts are (mostly) boys.

2. Boys often SMELL BAD (especially when they have been running around playing sweaty scouty games. Ewwww.)

3. Boys leave old bits of chewy under the seats.

4. They also leave **BOY GERMS** all over the wooden *barre* we hold onto when we are doing our *demi-pliés*. (Which is another fancy word for a type of knee-bending exercise.)

So anyway, we were all in the middle of our warm-up stretches when Mrs (I mean *Madame*) Fry announced that she had an important announcement to make. Of course we all wanted to know IMMEDIATELY what the important announcement was going to be. But Madame Fry said we had to wait until the end of class. And that she would only tell us if we had all worked really hard with NO SLACKING OFF.

So then we had to finish off our warm-up stretching, do all the knee-bendy *plié* things at the *barre*, and practise all our leaps and jumps and twirls across the floor (my favourite part) before we could find out. Mrs Radinsky (who is about 896 years old) played tinkly music on the piano (which is even older) while Madame Fry walked around the room putting our legs and arms in the right place or checking to see our backs were straight and our bottoms tucked in.

Sticking your bottom out in ballet is the WORST THING YOU CAN POSSIBLY DO.

WRONG ✗ **Right** ✓

Then she said we had to wait until we'd completed our warm-down stretches before she revealed her important announcement. By then of course everyone was getting really twitchy, busting to know what it was. There was Madame Fry telling us to be CALM, CALM, CALM, when actually we were all CRAZY, CRAZY, CRAZY, buzzing like little ballet bees trapped in a bottle. Especially Zoe and me. We LOVE important announcements (especially if they have anything to do with chocolate cake.)

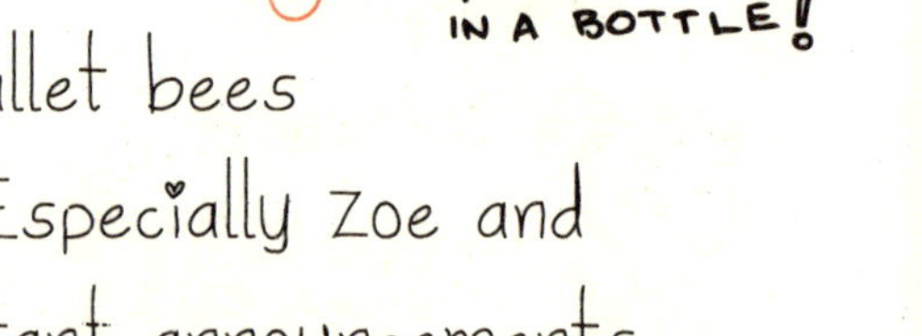

Then, finally, we stretched our last stretch and it was time! Madame Fry turned to us, her eyes shining like twin twinkly stars, and said:

'Everyone, I have something VERY VERY exciting to tell you.'

We all turned to each other, our eyes shining like ~~76~~ ~~92~~ a sky full of twinkly stars, wondering what the exciting thing might be.

Possible EXCITING things MADAME was about TO TELL US:

1. Our *École du Ballet* has been discovered by a famous movie producer, and we are all about to become famous movie stars.

2. A pop star wants us all to appear as dancers in his next video clip.

3. Mrs Radinsky is going to retire.

4. A ballet shoe company has decided to award us all ~~$500~~ $10,000 dance scholarships and give us ballet shoes for ever and ever.

5. An advertising company needs two **brilliant dancers** who look just like Zoe and me to appear in a TV commercial for chocolate cake.

And then Madame Fry told us **that** . . . .